A Note to Parents and Caregivers:

Read-it! Readers are for children who are just starting on the amazing road to reading. These beautiful books support both the acquisition of reading skills and the love of books.

The RED LEVEL presents familiar topics using common words and repeating sentence patterns.
The BLUE LEVEL presents new ideas using a larger vocabulary and varied sentence structure.
The YELLOW LEVEL presents more challenging ideas, a broad vocabulary, and wide variety in sentence structure.

When sharing a book with your child, read in short stretches, pausing often to talk about the pictures. Have your child turn the pages and point to the pictures and familiar words. And be sure to reread favorite stories or parts of stories.

There is no right or wrong way to share books with children. Find time to read with your child and pass on the legacy of literacy.

Adria F. Klein, Ph.D.
Professor Emeritus
California State University
San Bernardino, California

First American edition published in 2003 by
Picture Window Books
5115 Excelsior Boulevard
Suite 232
Minneapolis, MN 55416
1-877-845-8392
www.picturewindowbooks.com

First published in Great Britain by Franklin Watts, 96 Leonard Street, London, EC2A 4XD
Text © Maggie Moore 2001
Illustration © Paula Knight 2001

Printed in the United States of America.
1 2 3 4 5 6 08 07 06 05 04 03

Library of Congress Cataloging-in-Publication Data
Moore, Maggie.
  Little Red Riding Hood / written by Maggie Moore ; illustrated by Paula Knight.—1st
American ed.
     p. cm. — (Read-it! fairy tale readers)
  Summary: A retelling of the folktale in which a little girl meets a hungry wolf in the
forest while on her way to visit her grandmother.
  ISBN 1-4048-0064-6
  [1. Fairy tales. 2. Folklore—Germany.] I. Knight, Paula, ill. II. Little Red Riding Hood
English. III. Title. IV. Series.
  PZ8.M8038 Li 2003
   398.2'0943'02—dc21
  [E]   2002072256

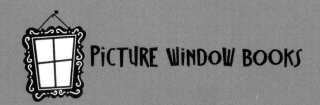

PICTURE WINDOW BOOKS

Little Red Riding Hood

Written by Maggie Moore

Illustrated by Paula Knight

Reading Advisors:
Adria F. Klein, Ph.D.
Professor Emeritus, California State University
San Bernardino, California

Ruth Thomas
Durham Public Schools
Durham, North Carolina

R. Ernice Bookout
Durham Public Schools
Durham, North Carolina

Picture Window Books
Minneapolis, Minnesota

Once upon a time, there was a girl called Little Red Riding Hood.

Little Red Riding Hood lived with her mother and father in a cottage in the forest.

In the forest lived a big, bad wolf.

Along the way, Little Red Riding Hood stopped to pick some flowers.

The big, bad wolf came up behind her.

"Hello, little girl," growled the big, bad wolf. "Where are you going?"

"I'm taking this cake to Grandmother," said Little Red Riding Hood.

The wolf had a plan.
He took a shortcut to
Grandmother's cottage
and knocked on the door.

"Hello, Grandmother," he growled. "It's Little Red Riding Hood."

That's not little Red
Riding Hood, thought
Grandmother. Quickly,
she hid in the closet.

The wolf opened the door
and went inside. "There's
no one here!" he grumbled.

The wolf put on Grandmother's nightgown and cap. Then he jumped into her bed.

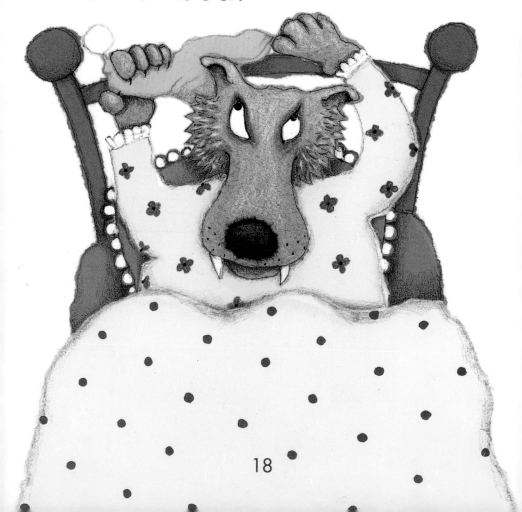

Soon, Little Red Riding Hood knocked on the cottage door.

"Come in, my dear," called the wolf, and he licked his lips.

"My, what big ears you have, Grandmother," said Little Red Riding Hood.

"All the better to hear you with," growled the wolf.

"My, what big eyes you have, Grandmother," said Little Red Riding Hood.

"All the better to see you with," growled the wolf.

"My, what big teeth you have, Grandmother," said Little Red Riding Hood.

"All the better to EAT YOU WITH!" roared the wolf as he jumped out of the bed.

Just then, a woodcutter walked past the cottage. He ran inside and chased the wolf away!

Little Red Riding Hood was safe.

Little Red Riding Hood heard knocking from inside the closet. She ran over and let Grandmother out.

"I'll never talk to strangers in the forest again!" said Little Red Riding Hood.

Red Level

The Best Snowman, by Margaret Nash 1-4048-0048-4
Bill's Baggy Pants, by Susan Gates 1-4048-0050-6
Cleo and Leo, by Anne Cassidy 1-4048-0049-2
Felix on the Move, by Maeve Friel 1-4048-0055-7
Jasper and Jess, by Anne Cassidy 1-4048-0061-1
The Lazy Scarecrow, by Jillian Powell 1-4048-0062-X
Little Joe's Big Race, by Andy Blackford 1-4048-0063-8
The Little Star, by Deborah Nash 1-4048-0065-4
The Naughty Puppy, by Jillian Powell 1-4048-0067-0
Selfish Sophie, by Damian Kelleher 1-4048-0069-7

Blue Level

The Bossy Rooster, by Margaret Nash 1-4048-0051-4
Jack's Party, by Ann Bryant 1-4048-0060-3
Little Red Riding Hood, by Maggie Moore 1-4048-0064-6
Recycled!, by Jillian Powell 1-4048-0068-9
The Sassy Monkey, by Anne Cassidy 1-4048-0058-1
The Three Little Pigs, by Maggie Moore 1-4048-0071-9

Yellow Level

Cinderella, by Barrie Wade 1-4048-0052-2
The Crying Princess, by Anne Cassidy 1-4048-0053-0
Eight Enormous Elephants, by Penny Dolan 1-4048-0054-9
Freddie's Fears, by Hilary Robinson 1-4048-0056-5
Goldilocks and the Three Bears, by Barrie Wade 1-4048-0057-3
Mary and the Fairy, by Penny Dolan 1-4048-0066-2
Jack and the Beanstalk, by Maggie Moore 1-4048-0059-X
The Three Billy Goats Gruff, by Barrie Wade 1-4048-0070-0